Pooh's
Fall Harvest

It was a crisp and cool fall day.
The leaves had just begun
to change colors.

6

Pooh and all his friends
gathered in Rabbit's garden.

"Hello, everyone," said Rabbit.
"Thank you for helping me
with my harvest!"

8

"Excuse me, Rabbit," said Pooh.

"We would love to help you

with your hardest,

but your hardest what?"

"No, Pooh," said Rabbit.

"I said 'harvest,' not 'hardest.'

It's fall—harvest season!"

"What is harvest season?"
asked Pooh.
"I only know winter,
spring, summer, and fall."

11

"Fall is the harvest season,"
said Christopher Robin.

"It's the time when
fruits and vegetables
in the garden become ripe."

"What does 'ripe' mean?"
asked Roo.

"It means
they are ready to eat,
dear," said Kanga.

15

"How do we tell
if they are ripe?" asked Piglet.
"Look for the vegetables
that look yummy," said Rabbit.

"They all look
yummy," said Eeyore.

17

Rabbit knelt down
to look among the leaves.
He saw a tiny squash.

"No, Eeyore, this one is too small.
It has some more growing to do."

Owl picked a different squash.
"Not too big, not too little,"
he said. "This one is ripe."

"That's right, Owl,"
said Rabbit.

21

"Rabbit, what about this apple?"
said Pooh. "It looks yummy."

22

Pooh sat on a branch.

He was pointing to an apple

on the branch above.

Pooh reached for the apple.

But he lost his balance

and fell . . .

into Christopher Robin's arms.

"You had better leave
the apple picking to me,"
said Tigger, with a laugh.

Rabbit had lots
of wonderful foods
to be gathered.

He had sweet potatoes,
tomatoes, pumpkins,
and corn.

After all of it was collected,
Rabbit said, "I have more
than enough food
for this winter's storage.

So I would like
to invite you all
to a harvest celebration!"

Everyone left,

so Rabbit could prepare.

When they returned,
a long table was
covered with food.

They each took a seat,
except Rabbit,
who stood at the head
of the table.

"Thank you for helping me
with the fall harvest," he said.
"You are wonderful friends!"

Can you match the words with the pictures?

leaves

Rabbit

potatoes

table

garden

Fill in the missing letters.

wi_ter

s_uash

ap_le

pu_pkin

R_o

Winnie the Pooh First Readers

Follow all the adventures
of Pooh and his friends!

Be Quiet, Pooh!

Bounce, Tigger, Bounce!

Eeyore Finds Friends

The Giving Bear

Happy Birthday, Eeyore!

Happy Valentine's Day, Pooh!

Pooh and the Storm That Sparkled

Pooh Gets Stuck

Pooh's Best Friend

Pooh's Christmas Gifts

Pooh's Easter Egg Hunt